JOSEPH O'CONNOR

THE · COMEDIAN

Joseph O'Connor was born in Dublin in 1963. He is the author of several best-selling novels: *Cowboys and Indians*, *Desperadoes*, *The Salesman*, *Inishowen* and *Star of the Sea*. He is also author of the popular Irish Male series. He has also written journalism, film and television scripts, as well as three plays, *Red Roses and Petrol*, *The Weeping of Angels* and *True Believers*.

GEMMA

Open Door

THE COMEDIAN
First published by GemmaMedia in 2009.

GemmaMedia
230 Commercial Street
Boston MA 02109 USA
617 938 9833
www.gemmamedia.com

Copyright © 2000, 2009 Joseph O'Connor

This edition of *The Comedian* is published by arrangement with New
Island Books Ltd.

Printed in the United States of America
Cover design by Artmark

13 12 11 10 09   1 2 3 4 5

ISBN: 978-1-934848-11-1

Cover design by Artmark

Library of Congress Preassigned Control Number (PCN) applied for

OPEN DOOR SERIES

An innovative program of original
works by some of our most
beloved modern writers and
important new voices. First designed
to enhance adult literacy in Ireland,
these books affirm the truth that
a story doesn't have
to be big to open the world.

Patricia Scanlan
Series Editor

OPEN DOOR

For A.G.
In fond memory

Chapter One

Back when I was seven years old, my family got to know this old woman. Her name was Agnes Bernadette Graham. She went to the same church we used to go to ourselves. The Holy Family Church in Glasthule, near Dun Laoghaire.

I don't know if you know Glasthule. You might not. To be honest, there's no real reason why you should. Unless you live there. Which you probably don't. Not may people do. Anyway it doesn't matter.

But Glasthule is a little place, a bit of

a village. You plug in your kettle and the street lights dim. That's what my father used to say. That was his favourite joke about Glasthule. But more about my father later.

Glasthule is more like some little town down the country than a part of Dublin. It's on the sea, which makes it nice. My father used to say the sea was good for people. He said the nearer people were to the sea, the more sane they were. He said that was why Dubliners were great people. And that was why people from the Midlands were all mad. They were too far from the sea. It wasn't good for them. It was why so many culchies came up to Dublin. They needed to get themselves nearer the sea.

He didn't really believe that at all. But it was the kind of thing he liked to say. It would annoy my mother because her family was from the country. Her family was from Athlone, County Westmeath. Athlone is in the exact dead centre of Ireland. It's about as far from the sea as you can *get* in Ireland. So he said that on purpose, just to annoy her. And it worked. It really did. She'd be annoyed.

I don't really know what it's like now. But when I was a kid in Glasthule you could often smell the sea in the air. You could smell it in the streets, even on your clothes. It was a town that was full of old biddies and stray dogs. Funny little shops that sold rashers and bottle of gas – dark little places that always looked closed. With dead flies and dead bees in the windows. There was a pub, the Eagle House. And a barber's, Paddy Connolly's. There used to be a little cinema too. But it was closed not too long ago and all boarded up. I think it was sold but I'm not sure.

Glasthule was where I grew up, but it's not where I live now. I don't even visit too much now. In some ways that's good. You have to move on in life. But in other ways it's a sad thing to pull up your roots. A place can get very deep into your bones. And when you leave it behind, you leave part of yourself.

My father's family lived in Glasthule for more than a hundred years. My great-great-grandfather went to live there in 1848. He was a young man then, from Francis Street in the oldest part of Dublin. He was a working man all his life. A stone cutter by trade. He helped to build Dun Laoghaire pier. He was part of the huge team of men who blasted the stones out of Dalkey Quarry to build that pier. They used sticks of dynamite to blast them out.

They would hammer a hole in a wall of rock with a chisel, then put in a stick of dynamite and blow it to pieces. Then they would cart the big stones down the hills to Dun Laoghaire through these special laneways they made beside the train tracks. The laneways are still there today. People in the area call those laneways "the metals". But nobody knows why. It's just a name.

Anyway, my great-great-grandfather married a Glasthule girl in 1852, the year the lighthouse on the pier was built. And it's a funny thing about that lighthouse, because that's exactly the spot where my father met my mother. It was one summer night in 1961. She was going for a walk down the pier with her friends when my father asked her if she had a light. He was a bit of a lad, my father was. A bit of a man for the ladies, they say. He shapes up to my mother and asks for a light. Then he gives her a wink. And he asks for a cigarette. Three months later they were husband and wife.

She often said she wished she hadn't gone walking the pier that night. Or that she hadn't stopped when he asked for the light.

It's a strange thing to think about, but it's true all the same. If she hadn't had a box of matches on her that night, I wouldn't be here to write this now. A box of matches can change history.

My father loved to walk the pier with me. All the way down to that lighthouse and back. On summer nights we did it often. It was a lovely walk, with the sun going down on the red water and the boats. Sometimes he would show me the little holes in the huge blocks of stone. From where the workmen had put in the sticks of dynamite all those years ago. When they were blasting the stones out of Dalkey Quarry.

Some of the blocks of stone were bigger than I was. Some were even bigger than my father. It was a funny feeling to look at a dynamite hole and to think that my own great-great-grandfather himself might have made it. His name was Paddy. Like my father's name, and my name. It made me feel very happy. It made me feel proud. To think one of my own family helped to build Dun Laoghaire pier. In fact he acted like he *owned* Dun Laoghaire pier. And he acted like he was the *king* of Glasthule.

But all my family have moved away from there now. The area changed. Lots of yuppies have moved in. The old shops are gone. The old families too. It gives me a strange feeling to think about it now. I find if I have to go down that way now, I try and avoid Glasthule altogether. A place can bring back very strong memories.

The year of my story is 1975. People like the Osmonds and the Bay City Rollers were in the charts. Where we lived, the teenage girls used to dress up like the Bay City Rollers. They'd have tartan shirts, tartan hats, tartan down the sides of their jeans. If they could have bought tartan knickers, they would have. I knew this one girl who lived down the street and everyone said she'd done just that. I don't know if it was true about her tartan knickers. But she certainly had tartan wallpaper on the covers of her school-books. That was the kind of family she had. The kind where the parents put wallpaper on your books. In mine, they didn't even put wallpaper on the walls.

You'd see the Bay City Rollers on the television. They'd be in interesting places like Glasgow or Japan. With girls screaming at them and going spare and singing:

B.A.Y
B.A.Y
B.A.Y
C.I.T.Y.
With an R.O.L.L.
E.R.S.
Bay City Rollers are the best!

I thought the girls were sad cows. I really did. Imagine getting so worked up about a shower of eejits in tartan. Apart from the Bay City Rollers, and *Starsky and Hutch*, it's hard to remember what else was going on. There was trouble in Northern Ireland, I suppose. Probably there were bombs going off. Petrol was scarce a lot of the time. The country wasn't doing well.

Anyway, where was I? Lately I find that I tend to forget things. Oh yes. The year was 1975. That's right. And that turned out to be a very big year for my family. Although we didn't know at the time that it would be. It was the year my mother ran away to England. All sorts of things got turned upside down. It really was one hell of a year. And when it was over nothing was the same.

Chapter Two

My parents weren't happily married. My father often used to joke about it. "Me and the wife have had nine wonderful years," he'd say. "Only trouble is, we've been married fourteen."

He had all sorts of jokes about his marriage. He never got tired of telling them either. "Me and the wife were happy once. The only problem is – then we met." All the old biddies in Glasthule used to love him. I don't think they knew his marriage really wasn't good. They thought he was only messing about it. He'd pull faces and tell them jokes. They'd laugh when they'd see him. They'd fall around laughing.

"Here he is," they'd say. "Here's the comedian."

And my father used to love it when they said that. It really gave him a big kick. He'd put on a silly face or a smile. "Marriage is a great institution," he'd say. "But who wants to live in a bleedin' institution?"

Most people have a dream in life. My father's was to be a comedian. He loved to tell jokes and to make people laugh. I think that was his favourite thing. He was never happier than when he was doing that. I think he would have liked to do that full-time. If his life had turned out differently, maybe he would have. In those days there was a television programme called *The Comedians*. It was on quite late on a Saturday night. If my father and mother weren't fighting, my father used to watch it. He'd have a beer and watch it, laughing his head off. He had a really loud laugh, like some kind of donkey. Sometimes when my mother was gone to bed, he'd let me sneak down and watch it with him. There were comedians like Les Dawson and Jimmy Tarbuck on the programme. Tom O'Connor and Tommy Cooper. Little and Large. Cannon and Ball. Another one was Dave Allen. My father liked Dave Allen a lot. I think he was his hero, really. He liked watching Dave Allen because he was from Dublin. I liked watching him because one of his fingers was missing.

"Look," he'd say when Dave Allen was on. "Look at your man, Son. He has it made. Over in England, on the pig's back. Earning millions for telling jokes. The women hanging out of him.

A man with nine fingers. Holy God, what a life."

People were always telling my father he was funny. People in Glasthule said that to him very often. Once a month there was a talent night in the Eagle House. There was a prize of twenty pounds for the winner. Ten pounds for second place. In 1975, that was big money. Everyone said if my father entered it and told his jokes, he'd win. He'd win for sure. No doubt about it. Everyone said that, except for my mother. But he never did enter it. I don't know why.

He and my mother really didn't get on at all. I never found out about the reason, but they just didn't. He drank a bit, but it was more than that. They didn't have a lot in common. Maybe they got married too young, who knows? He was eighteen; she was nineteen. You change a lot in your early twenties. Maybe they just grew apart as they grew up.

They look very happy in their wedding-day photos. A happy couple, smiling and kissing. I still have one of those photos somewhere. They look a bit older than eighteen and nineteen. It's an odd thing and I don't understand it. But people did tend to look older in those days.

"I never knew what happiness was, until I got married. And then, of course, it was too bloody late." That was another one of my father's jokes. He loved that one. He really did. He'd be killed laughing. He'd nearly wet himself.

One night Dave Allen was on the *Late Late Show*. He said the secret of comedy was never to laugh yourself. To tell jokes without laughing at all. To keep a straight face when everyone was laughing around you. But my father could never do that, no matter how he tried. He laughed at his own jokes. He just didn't care.

My father was a breadman around Dun Laoghaire. That was his work. Delivering bread. His round was from Dun Laoghaire up to Ballybrack. All around the new estates in Sallynoggin and Monkstown Farm. The king of the road. That's what he said about himself. "Paddy Plunkett, the king of the road. A job where you travel is a great thing."

He had a small van that was run by electricity. Sometimes in the summer he would take me out in it. He wasn't supposed to. It was against the rules. He would have got into trouble if the bakery ever found out. Though I never knew why he would have got into trouble. Because it wasn't as if his van was dangerous. It was so slow. It was like a toy. "There wouldn't be enough power in that yoke to work a train-set." That's what my father used to say. And he'd laugh to himself. And he'd pull a face. "The king of the road. In my speed machine. But, sure it'll have to do. Till I get the Rolls Royce."

I loved going out on the bread-round with my father. I often did that in the school holidays or on a Saturday. He'd let me help him carry the trays of cakes and bread. He'd carry the big ones. I'd carry the smaller ones. "Look at us," he'd say. "Little and Large."

It was a good feeling to be helping my father. The old biddies would sometimes give me money. I liked the lovely warm smell of the hot bread. It made me feel warm too. It was a nice safe smell. It made me feel happy just to think about it.

Sometimes, late at night, I'd be listening to them fight each other downstairs. And I'd be crying to myself. I'd be afraid, I suppose. She'd be saying she was going to go away. Sometimes, he'd be saying that too. I would sit on the top stair and cry while I listened. Sometimes Helen or Sheila would come out of their room and sit beside me. They'd be crying as well, even more than me.

I'd hear my parents smashing the plates or the glasses downstairs. I'd hear them screaming all sorts of things. Pushing each other around the kitchen. And what I'd do then – I'd get back into bed and pull the covers up over my head. And I'd try to think about the lovely happy smell. Often I would dream about it. Sometimes I still do. The lovely smell of hot fresh bread.

There were two boys and two girls in

our family. I was the eldest child. So I was the only one of us who could remember happier times. The times when my mother and father didn't fight each other.

Another thing I could remember was praying to Jesus to send my brother Rory to us. He was the youngest. I prayed for him to be born. I think I was sick to death of having sisters. I wanted to have a brother so I could teach him how to play football. Helen and Sheila didn't like football much. No girls did, back in those days.

Rory and me used to play football often. We played football out on the street. He was Chelsea, I was Man United. I was Brazil, he was Germany. Sometimes he wanted to be Brazil, but I wouldn't ever let him. I was Brazil. That was the rule.

It's funny, because Rory and me never see each other now. He got into trouble a few years back. He got mixed up with a bad crowd in town. There were drugs involved. He did things he shouldn't have done. There's no point in talking about it now.

I'm not saying it's up to me to judge him. I love him still. I just can't be around him. It would wreck your head to be around him. I wouldn't even know where he lives any more. I wouldn't even know if he is alive right now. It's a sad thing to have bad blood with your brother. But me and Rory do. And it won't change now.

Still, back when we were only kids I was very fond of him. I prayed that my mother would have a baby boy and she did. I was thrilled when she did. I really was. A baby brother. What a gas. An answer to my prayers. I used to tell him: "If it wasn't for me, pal, you'd never have got here. So you're Germany. So shut your gob."

Chapter Three

The first day we met Agnes Graham was a Sunday. A very cold Sunday in winter of 1975. It was the kind of day where your breath turns into steam. Or smoke, if you are a child. You are at the age when you see magic in things.

We were just standing in front of Glasthule Church on that freezing morning. The five of us. My father and Helen and Sheila and me, and little Rory in my father's arms. We were blowing on our thumbs to keep our hands warm. I suppose we were thinking about what we could do.

Because although we were too young to be able to admit it, we didn't want to go home. We didn't want that at all. This was because the worst fights in our house were always on a Sunday. And they always ended with my father putting on his jacket and leaving the house. And not coming back until it was late.

My father looked at me that cold Sunday morning. I could see by the look on his face that he knew what I was thinking. His lips were kind of cracked and pale. He kept chewing at the skin there while he stared around the place. I wondered what he was staring at, exactly. He looked like he was waiting for some strange thing to start happening.

"Daddy," said Sheila. "I'm cold."

"Well, I know you're cold, Teapot," my father said. "But think of the poor black people in Africa. In the desert. The backsides roasted halfway off them. Think how much they'd like to be here in Glasthule now."

"I don't care about the black people in Africa," she said.

"Do you know how hot it is in Africa?" he said. "It's so hot in Africa, right, that you sweat so much you have to carry yourself home in a bottle."

"I wish I was there now, instead of here," she said.

My father laughed softly. "So do I," he said. "If you want to know the gospel truth."

A sad look came over Sheila's face then. She could look very sad sometimes when she was a kid. It would break your heart to look at her sometimes. She wasn't a kid who could hide her feelings.

"Will I tell you a joke?" he said. "To cheer you up?"

"No," she said. "I don't want to hear a joke."

"Once upon a time there was three bears," he said. "And now there's bloody millions of them."

My father laughed. But Sheila didn't.

We stood in front of the church until all the people had gone home. Until the man who sold the newspaper had packed up his stall. The young priest came out the front gates of the church. He was kind of hugging himself because it was so cold. He went in next door to his little house. I could see him in there. In his front room. He was sitting at a fire. He was eating his lunch. And I remember wishing that I was a priest who had a little house. A place where there'd be no parents, no brothers, no sisters. Nobody to love. Nobody to cause you any trouble. I decided I would be a priest when I grew up.

"Ah, to blazes with it," my father said. "I feel like a bit of gas today. Come on, we'll get the bus down to Bray or Greystones. Some culchie place where they eat their young."

"Do you mean it?" we said.

"Course I mean it. Come on."

We thought this was great. Now we wouldn't have to go home until five or six o' clock. Now there wouldn't be as much time for them to fight each other. I remember feeling so happy then. Because it might be a Sunday that would turn out all right.

The wind blew my father's hat off. I ran back through the church gates to get it for him. And that was when I saw something weird.

At first, to be honest, I thought she

was dead. Down beside the wall of the church, beside the big black plastic bin where they kept the holy water, I saw this little old woman.

She was lying on the ground, flat on her back. Her arms were stretched out, as though she was Jesus. Her eyes were closed. Her legs were thin and very crooked. Her skin was white. She was lying so still. I can remember thinking, this old woman is dead. What should we do?

Beside her on the ground was an empty Coca-Cola bottle. It was lying there on the smooth black ice.

"Oh my God," my father said. "That poor old biddy is after slipping."

My father walked over carefully to where the old woman was. He put his hands in his pockets. He nodded his head. He looked over his shoulder, but nobody was coming to help him. He stared down at her, and he said, "HELLO, hello?" in this kind of funny frightened voice. As though this old woman was some kind of wild animal who might wake up and chew a lump out of him.

We crept up behind him. It was fun seeing him scared. For a while we just stood there, laughing a bit. I could feel my heart beginning to pound. Then I stopped in front of my father. I saw the old woman's head. It was bleeding. It turned, on the ground. It looked up at us.

Nobody said anything for a good long while. Then I took another step forward. "So," I went, "what is your name?"

"Love, my name is Agnes," she goes. "And I am the Lamb of God."

And then she started to cry like a baby. Well, I think she just got frightened all of a sudden. She seemed to be confused, all shaken up. She didn't seem to know where she was. She opened her beak to cry, and her false teeth nearly fell out. They were horrible. They really were. She put her hand on her mouth and cried like a baby.

My father got down on his knees beside her. He put his arms around her and gave her a hug. Then he stroked the back of her head. "Where am I?" she said. "What's after happening to me now?"

"You're safe now, Missus," my father said. "You're at the church. You're grand. Nothing bad can happen to you here."

Slowly we helped Agnes up on her feet. Her old black coat smelled of candles and cat's pee. She looked around the place, kind of sniffing. Her eyes had little lines of red in them.

What she told my father was this: she had been stretching up to get some holy water out of the bin when she turned her ankle on the ice. "You poor auld thing," my father said. "You have to be on the look-out for that in this weather."

My father started to fuss then. He put his hand on Agnes's forehead. He made her count her fingers. He said he wanted to get a doctor or take Agnes to a hospital. But she shook her head and said she was fine now. She kept looking at my father. She gazed into his face. It was like my father was someone that she knew, but whose name she couldn't remember.

"There is one thing you could do for me," she said then. She picked up her empty Coca-Cola bottle. She waved the bottle in front of herself. And she nodded in the direction of the holy water bin.

"Say no more," my father said. He took the bottle from her, reached into the bin and filled it up. She smiled when he gave the bottle back to her. And I noticed for some reason my father was blushing. "Now, Pet," he said. "You're sucking the diesel." He rubbed his cold hands on the front of his coat. His hand and fingers were blue with the cold.

"I am," she said. "I'm laughing now."

We walked Agnes home that day. She lived in a block of flats called Glasthule Buildings. It was on a little narrow street, in behind the Forum Cinema. The street was dirty. There was a burnt-out car turned on its side. Someone had spray-painted UP THE PROVOS on a wall. And THIN LIZZY RULES OK. And MARY MOORE WEARS TARTAN KNICKERS.

Agnes said she'd like to invite us in

for a cup of tea. But the flat was all upside down, so she couldn't today. But she might another day, she said. My father said that was fine. But I was disappointed. I would have loved to see inside the home of a strange, smelly, funny old woman.

From then on, I used to look forward to seeing Agnes at Mass every Sunday. Sheila said Agnes was a witch, but I paid no attention to that. I liked Agnes. She was full of strange stories. But Sheila didn't like her one bit. Sheila said Agnes was a dirty cannibal. She said there was a good reason Agnes wouldn't allow us into her flat. She said Agnes killed people in there and ate them. She said Agnes made hot-dogs out of dead men's fingers. I know that wasn't true, of course. But I would have been afraid to go in there on my own.

Little by little, we got to know Agnes

well. She was always curious about our lives. She'd ask you questions. She'd want to know how we were doing in school. What we wanted to be when we grew up.

Sometimes she was curious about our mother too. She asked about my mother a lot, in those early days when we met her first.

"She must be proud of such a lovely family," she'd say. "She must thank God to have you all."

My father would go a bit quiet when she said that. And then he'd say, "Well we're both proud, Rita and me too. When they're not being a shower of cheeky bowsies."

He told Agnes my mother preferred to get Mass in Dun Laoghaire or Sallynoggin. And we never let on, but that wasn't true. The truth was my mother had stopped going to Mass by then. The way things turned out, she never did meet Agnes. That's a pity. I always thought they would have got on. I remember once telling my mother about Agnes. I said my father was very kind to her.

"Oh, is he?" she said, in a strange, angry voice. "Well your father should realise that charity begins at home."

But later that night my mother came into me and Rory's room. She sat on my bed for a while and she smoked a cigarette. She said she didn't mean what she said about my father. She said my father was a good man at heart. And she didn't want me to turn against him. In case I wouldn't want to get married myself when I grew up. I told her I didn't ever want to get married. "I want to stay with you, Mammy," I said.

She laughed. "You won't always feel that way," she said.

"I will so," I said. "Why can't I marry you?"

"Because one day you'll meet some lovely girl," she said. "And you'll fall for her."

"I won't," I said.

"You will," she told me. "That's what happens. That's what makes the world go around. When you fall in love, that's a wonderful thing."

"Like you and Daddy," I said to her then.

She looked away. She took a drag on her cigarette.

"Yes," she said. "Like me and Daddy."

Chapter Four

My mother wasn't religious at all. She said religion was all lies and rubbish. She'd talk about it very bitterly. But one thing you could say about my mother was this – at least she hated all religions equally.

Agnes was different, of course. But there was one odd thing about her. She was very holy, but she didn't like priests. She didn't like them one little bit. She said priests were only fools and chancers who were living it up like the Queen of England. I used to hear her during the sermon at Mass. She'd be sitting in the seats behind us, scoffing to herself and clicking her tongue. She said things like, "That's a good one coming from him." Or, "A lot he'd know about the will of God." The poor priest would be scarlet. People would be laughing.

Agnes had never married herself. When we asked her why not, she used to tell us that she was still waiting for the right fella. Then she'd rock with laughter, wiping her eyes. "God forgive me," she'd say. "I'm a terrible rip."

One day she showed me a picture of the Sacred Heart. With his eyes all mad and a Georgie Best hair-do. And his chest all open and bleeding down his shirt. "Do you see himself?" she said to me. "That's the only fella I'll ever have."

Other times she used to say that all men were the same, and she wasn't one bit sorry to be on her own. I think she had a bit of a thing for my father though. She was a flirty thing sometimes. She really was. "If only you were forty years older," she'd say. "I'd give you a right run for your money, so I would. I like a man with a bit of go in him. Not them fellas who think they only have it for stirring their tea."

"Agnes Graham!" he'd say, pretending to be shocked. "You're an awful woman, Agnes Graham. Throwing yourself at me like that. And me a happily married man. You're an awful auld hoor, so you are, Agnes Graham."

She would laugh like a nutcase then, and so would he. And we'd all laugh too. Me and Helen and Sheila. Even though we didn't actually know what a "hoor" was.

The one night we were sitting on the landing, listening to them fighting each other downstairs. And I heard my father call my mother that name.

"You're a useless drunken bastard," she screamed.

"And you're an evil hoor," he roared. "I curse the day I ever met you!"

She started crying then. So did he. A door slammed hard, I remember that. It was like a gun going off, it was so loud. It was like a blast of dynamite going off.

I could hear them, crying downstairs, in different rooms. And I knew what the word meant then all right.

And I promised myself that when I grew up I would never use a word like that to anyone. I did not realise that when people are in love they can say terrible things. And that people will use a word as a weapon. A word can go into your heart like a bullet. But a bullet goes right through you, and a word stays inside. It stays in your heart till it turns your heart sour. But I didn't know anything about that at the time. That's because I was a child. I was too young to know.

We never found out what age Agnes was. "Sixteen," she'd say, whenever we asked her. "Sweet sixteen and never been kissed." Oh, she'd fall around the place at that one. She'd laugh until she went red in the face. But my father told me once that she must be at least eighty. Because she could actually remember Queen Victoria dying. That was back in 1901. Agnes was only a little girl then. But I couldn't picture her as a little girl, no matter how hard I tried. In my own mind, Agnes had always been old.

Agnes had this big thing about the devil. She was a bit bonkers, the poor old thing. She was a couple of bottles short of a six-pack. That's the way my father put it. She talked about the devil all the time. She told us what she did with all the holy water she got from the church. She used it, she said, to scare off the devil. She poured it all over everything in her house, to keep the devil away from her. She held up her Coca-Cola bottle and shook it hard. "Oh, this is the real thing, right enough," she cackled. "I always keep a bottle of this in the house. For whenever his nibs comes calling on me. And if that doesn't work, I show him me special picture. Of my own true love. My own little Charlie."

Her favourite possession. Her signed photo of Charlie Haughey. Taken the day he came to look for votes in Glasthule. One arm around Agnes. The other around the parish priest. Terry Keane behind him, looking bored out of her tree.

She drenched her clothes and her sheets with holy water. She drank it, cooked her food in it, watered her plants with it. And whenever she washed herself – which Sheila said wasn't very often – she filled her bath with it, up to the brim. She sprinkled it over her furniture and up and down the stairs. She said she could see the devil's eyes at night, coming in through the curtains. Little bright eyes like Gay Byrne, but a voice like fingernails scraping on a blackboard. He was coming to drag her off to Hell. He was coming to punish her for being such a sinner.

My father didn't like when she went on like this. "Don't be going on like that now, Agnes," he'd say. "Don't be giving the kiddies bad dreams."

"It's true," she'd say. "Child, woman or grown man, it's all the same to the prince of darkness."

"There's no such place as Hell," he'd say. "And if there is, it couldn't be worse than Athlone."

"There is so a Hell," she'd tell him. "And what's more, I've seen it."

"When?" I said. "When did you see Hell?"

"Jesus showed it to me," she said. "A great big lake of fire and ice. And the awful screeches of the poor sinners."

"Don't mind her at all," my father said. "She's only messing. She's joking. She's a right comedian. Aren't you, Agnes?"

"Oh am I?" she said, very angry now. "A comedian, is it? Well, I believe in my religion, thank you. That the English pagans tried to beat out of us. And on the last day of the world, we'll see who's laughing. When you're being roasted on the hobs of Hell!"

My father told us not to mind her. He said Agnes was only a bloody madwoman. He said Agnes should be locked up in a home for loonies. And the next week at Mass he didn't speak to her. I felt sorry for Agnes that day. She was standing beside the holy water bin, all alone. She was looking at us when she thought my father couldn't see her.

The Sunday after that she came up to us outside the church. She had four chocolate biscuits, wrapped up in an old piece of *The Irish Press*. She said she had missed us all very much. She said that she had been praying for us all. My father looked cross. But when he saw the biscuits all wrapped up in the paper, he looked a bit ashamed. And then he smiled at Agnes. And he gave her a little hug. He said that we had missed her too.

"You can walk me home, so," she said to my father. "You can beat away the men. All my fans. They have me driven mad, so they do."

Things went on like that for a while. Nothing very important happened with Agnes and us. We would meet her outside the church on a Sunday. Help her fill up her bottle of holy water. We would talk for a while, have a natter. Sometimes we'd go for a walk down to the sea. We had to go slowly, though, because Agnes couldn't walk very fast.

We would sometimes buy ice-creams in this place called Teddy's near the public baths. We would sit on a bench and pass the time. My father would give her a few little cakes or a sliced pan that was left over from his bread-round. One time, for some reason, she cried when he did that.

After we had left her home, I asked my father why Agnes had cried. He thought about it for a long time before he spoke.

"It's hard to help a proud person," he told me. "Especially if the person is a lady. But you should always help them anyway, if you can. Because you never know when you might need help yourself in life. And you should never judge another person. Not until you've walked a mile in their shoes."

"But why can't she buy her own bread?" I asked him. "Is she poor?"

He laughed to himself, in a quiet way. "Well," he said. "She's not rich."

"Are we poor?" I asked him then.

"Don't be saying that," he said, "when we have enough never to be hungry or cold. That's more than a lot of people in this world have."

And again he thought for a long time. "It's a terrible thing to be lonely in life," he said. "You could have all the money in the whole world. But where would it get you, if you've nobody to love you? Nobody is poor if they have that."

"Do you love Mammy?" I asked him then.

"Yes," he said. "Of course I do."

"Then why are you always fighting?" I asked him.

He looked away from me and out at the sea. He put his hand up over his eyes, as though the sun was in them. When he looked back at me he was trying to smile. Though his eyes weren't smiling. Only his mouth.

"That's only a little game we play," he said. "Don't you worry about anything. That's only messing."

"But what kind of a game is that?" I asked him.

"It's like when you and Rory are playing Cowboys and Indians," he said. "You pretend to be fighting but you don't mean it."

I couldn't think of anything to say.

"Or it's like when you're playing football," he said. "Your mammy's Germany. And I'm Brazil."

I can see him saying that, as though it was yesterday. I can still see the way he was trying to smile.

Chapter Five

Agnes just became a part of our lives. We got used to her and she got used to us. After a while, it was like we had always known her. She would give us holy pictures on our birthdays. She would always tell us to give our mother her regards.

Sometimes I would think about Agnes at night. They'd be screaming and roaring downstairs, until late. They'd be breaking the place up. Throwing the cups. I would wonder how much Agnes really knew about us.

way, a great man. In his work as a breadman he had helped a lot of people. He was known all the way from Dun Laoghaire up to Ballybrack. From Monkstown Farm over to Sallynoggin. The king of the road. That's what he was. He was known for his kindness everywhere.

Nobody was saying he was a perfect saint. Nobody was saying he never made a mistake. But the man who had never made a mistake never made anything. A man like that wasn't a man at all. Paddy Plunkett always had a kind word for the lonely person. The person who was down on their luck, in trouble. To many people, before his own bad luck began, Paddy Plunkett was much more than a breadman.

"Paddy, like Jesus, did miracles with bread," the priest said.

"And with wine," somebody

If she really was a witch who could see into the secret part of our lives.

I remember my eighth birthday fell on a Sunday. After Mass that day, Agnes took me to one side. She gave me a little parcel, wrapped in blue and gold paper. It was a set of black rosary beads. They had the words "MOTHER IN HEAVEN" on the medal.

"Thank you very much, Agnes," I said. Although secretly I felt like choking her with them. Because I wasn't very interested in rosary beads. She smiled at me. She touched my face with her fingers.

"You're the eldest," she said. "That's a cross, love. I know that and Jesus knows it too." The way she looked at me made it hard to look away.

"Pray to the Holy Family," she whispered. "They'll always help you when you're feeling sad."

"I will, Agnes," I said. And for some reason I wanted to cry.

"Never forget that God loves you," she said. "And things will always turn out for the best, you'll see. Because God never sends you a cross you can't carry."

Agnes kissed me then. She gave me a hug. She said I was handsome. Like my father was handsome. She said when I grew up I would break somebody's heart.

I remember another special day. It was in the autumn of 1975. The 27th of October, in fact. We all went on the bus to Bray after Mass. My father and me with Sheila and Helen and Rory. And Agnes. We left my mother at home. We always left my mother at home on Sundays.

Agnes was so excited about going to Bray. Her face went all purple. You would swear she was going to New York or Las Vegas.

It was a wonderful day. The sky was clear and the sea was blue. All along the sea-front the bumper cars were rattling. There was a sweet smell of candy floss in the air. We bought orange ice-pops and looked at the waves for a while. Agnes said the waves were the souls of the angels who God really loved. She said God let them dance around on the sea, to say thank you to them for being so good.

"Some bloody thank you," Sheila said. Under her breath.

We walked all the way up Bray Head. My father kept saying we had walked far enough. But Agnes was mad keen to go all the way up. She wanted to see the big black cross at the top. By the time we got half the way up, Agnes had to stop every few yards for a rest. She was huffing and puffing like an old train. Her face was bright red and she was gasping. People stared at my father. They pointed at him. I think they thought he was forcing this poor old lady to climb all the way up this terrible hill. They didn't see it was all her idea.

When we got to the top she kissed the big cross. The she started to sing. Not just to herself. I mean not just quietly. But at the top of her voice. Giving it the lash. Like she just didn't care.

Georgie Best
Superstar
Walks like a woman
And he wears a bra!

I felt so ashamed. People were laughing at us. On the way back down I walked by myself. I didn't want people to know I knew Agnes.

"That was the best day ever," she

said, when we dropped her home. "That was really great gas now."

"We'll do it again, Agnes," my father said.

But that wasn't true. Not the way things turned out. As we walked up the hill and home that day, my father didn't know that the days like this would never happen again. Everything in life was about to change.

When we got back home the house was empty. That was strange. My mother never went out on a Sunday. In fact, by then, she hardly went out at all. I think it was Sheila who found the note in the kitchen. "Daddy," she said. "Mammy's gone away."

"Don't be silly," he laughed. "She's gone out for a walk."

"No," said Sheila. "No, you're wrong."

She gave him the note she had

found on the table. She was crying now. Her face all squeezed up. The note said that my mother had taken enough. "I will always love you all," it said. "But I just can't go on with a life like this."

My father stared at this note for a long time. He was holding it very lightly in his hands. As though the piece of paper was on fire. He sat down on the stairs and he read it again. And after a while he looked up at us.

"That's only a joke," he said. "Don't mind it." He rolled the note up into a ball. He put it in his pocket and went into the toilet. He stayed in there for a long time.

I was not very upset. I knew my father was, but to be honest I could not see why. All I could see was that now there would be no more fights. When you are the age that I was then, you don't see the pain of being left. Or the pain of leaving either. Because there is pain there too. But you are just too young to know about these things.

When Sheila and Helen had stopped crying that night, my father went out to get chips and burgers. He had gone for a very long time. When he came back he had a smell of beer on his breath. He told us that "a really gas thing" had happened. He had run into a friend of my mother up in the chip shop. She had told him my mother was just gone away on a little holiday. She had gone down the country to see her relations. She would be back in a few days' time, he said. Everything would be grand then. Everything would be fine.

"So you see?" he smiled. "I told you there was nothing to worry about." He put the chips out onto plates and he looked me in the eye.

Chapter Six

A week went by and she didn't come back. Soon it was two weeks, and then a month. Before very long Christmas came. We got great presents. The best presents we ever had. Rory and me got brand new football boots. The girls got dresses and dolls and toys. I just didn't know how Santa Claus could afford them. We'd always been told before that Santa Claus was poor. But that year, it seemed, Santa Claus was rich.

Christmas passed. The new year

began. Still there was no word at all of my mother.

Sometimes at night I would look out my window. My father would be standing out on the path. He'd be looking up and down the street, as though he was waiting for somebody to come along. One time I asked him who he was waiting for. "Oh," he said. "Just this man I know. Don't you worry about it. Everything's fine."

And then my father started coming home early from work. He wanted to be there when we came home from school. He would bring home chips for our dinner. Some days he'd bring home pizza instead. Then my father started learning to cook, out of a book he got one Saturday in Dun Laoghaire. He burned every single pot in the house. Sheila said our mother was never coming home now.

"You don't have to come home early," I told him one day. "We can look after ourselves."

"Don't worry about that," he'd say. "I like to come home early."

One day I was coming home from school when a strange thing happened. I turned into the street and got a surprise. Outside our house, a thin man in a suit was talking to my father. I had seen this thin man before. I knew he worked at the bakery with my father. I knew he was my father's boss.

Beside the thin man was a big fat policeman. The policeman's neck was thicker than his head. As I got closer I could hear that the bakery man and my father were having an argument.

"Ah, now," the policeman said to my father. "Don't be talking like that now. There's no need at all for that class of language."

Suddenly my father took a step forward and pushed the man from the bakery. "Don't you *dare* say that to me ever again, pal," he said. "Or I'll put you through that window, so I will."

He went into the house and slammed the door. The policeman and the man in the suit looked down at me.

"There you are," the policeman said.

"What's the matter?" I asked him.

The thin man and the policeman looked at each other. The thin man said something quietly and walked away in a hurry.

The policeman sighed and he rubbed my head.

"You're a great little man, aren't you?" he said. "What are you going to be when you grow up?"

I said I didn't know.

"Would you like to be a policeman?" he asked me.

"No," I said.

"Would you not like that? To be a policeman and catch robbers? I could put in a word for you so I could. There's a place for a big strong lad like you."

"My father says all policemen are culchies," I said.

The policeman laughed. "Does he now? He's a gas man, isn't he? A right comedian."

"I want to be a priest," I said.

He looked at me in a funny way. It was like I had said I was Jesus or something. There was an awful smell of stew off him.

"Well," he said. "That's a great thing for a boy to want to be."

He gave me ten pence and went away. The big fat culchie. He walked like a duck.

I went into the house after my father. He was in the kitchen. His shirt was off.

He was just standing there, in his vest and trousers. He didn't say anything. Not one word. He got a pint of milk out of the fridge and drank it down in three huge gulps. A strange thought came into my head, then. He didn't look like our father any more. He wiped his face with his vest. He leaned his hand on the kitchen table. He looked around the kitchen as if he had never been there before. He looked like a very tired man who needed to sleep for a week.

"Why was that man from the bakery here?" I asked him.

He said nothing. So I asked him again.

He still said nothing. He looked frightened and young. But after a while he gave a laugh.

"That man was only messing," he said. "He was only having the crack. That was only a mess we were having. That's nothing for you to worry about.

Come on out now and we'll go for a walk on the pier."

We walked all the way down to the end of the pier. Down to the lighthouse at the very end. But my father was in a quiet mood that evening. He didn't seem to want to talk. We sat on the benches, down near the lighthouse. The six o'clock boat was leaving for England. We watched it sailing out of the harbour. There were people on the deck, walking up and down. They all looked like they were having a great time.

"Were you ever in England?" I asked my father.

"I was going to go once," he said. "When I was younger."

"Why didn't you?"

He took out a cigarette and lit it.

"I might yet," he said, in a quiet way.

"I wouldn't like that," I told him. "I wouldn't like you to go away."

He didn't look at me. He reached out and took my hand. We sat like that for a while. Not saying anything. While the beam of the lighthouse swept over the water.

"Is Santa Claus real?" I asked my father.

"Of course he is," my father said.

One day not long after that I found a letter in his bedroom. It was from the bakery. It said they knew that things were difficult at home. But the money he had taken would have to be given back right away. Or else there would be very serious trouble.

I don't know what happened after that. But when my father came home to the house the next afternoon, he never went back to work again.

Chapter Seven

One Sunday morning in March, Agnes didn't come to Mass. We looked all over the church for her, but she wasn't there. So after Mass we didn't bother to get the newspapers. Instead we went to call in to Agnes, just to make sure she was feeling all right.

Outside Agnes's door in Glasthule Buildings there were four bottles of milk on the step. One of the bottles was cracked. The birds had pecked the foil off the tops. My father rang the doorbell. Nobody came. That didn't matter, he said. Agnes was a bit deaf.

He pressed the doorbell again. Hard. Three times. He rapped on the door with his knuckles. But still nobody came.

My father banged on the window with his wedding ring. The curtains were closed. He turned and smiled at us. Then he banged the glass again, so hard that I thought he might break it and get us into trouble.

There were boot-boys standing against the wall, just looking at us. One of them had a radio under his arm. It was playing a song by Thin Lizzy. The boy with the radio had his eyes closed. He was shaking his head in time to the music. The other boys just kept staring at us.

Sheila said she wanted to go home. She said she didn't like being here one bit. I told her to shut up.

My father bit his lip. He walked up

and down outside the house. He was running his fingers through his hair. And all of a sudden my father looked like a child. Or a man who is badly lost in his life. A man in a fairy-tale, lost in the forest.

"Something's wrong," he said. "I think something's wrong," He punched the wall of the house, gently. He ran his fingers around the inside of his collar. He stared at the milk bottles in a line outside Agnes's door. He stared at his watch. Then he stared at me.

He was trying to smile, but he didn't look happy. Suddenly, he put his hand on my shoulder and told me to listen. I had to go and knock on all the doors in the street. I had to find someone who had a telephone. I had to tell them to ring for the police.

All sorts of things were going through my head. I walked up the street, knocking on all the doors. Finally I found a woman who was in. She called her husband out from the kitchen. She told him to run to the pub and get help. I ran down the street after him. I was trying to keep up. And now there was a crowd of people outside of Agnes's house.

Sheila was sitting on the path, with her coat up over her head. Helen was trying to look through the window. Rory was crawling around in the gutter. As I walked over, I saw one man in the crowd take off his hat. I heard a sound coming from Agnes's hall. It was a sound I knew. It was a sound of a group of people praying.

I pushed my way in through the smashed front door. The smell nearly made me sick. From the top of the stairs I saw a big black cat staring down at me. It had bright yellow eyes.

It licked its lips. It seemed to be yawning.

My father was standing in the front room with his back to me. His right hand was holding his shoulder. His other hand was pressing a hanky over his mouth and nose. A small, scared-looking man who I didn't know was standing beside my father. He had an axe in his hand. His face was white. His lips were moving. But no sound was coming from his mouth.

The floor was thick with dirty old newspapers. The room stank of rot and dirt. There was a picture of the Virgin Mary on the wall. She was smiling and wearing a long blue cloak.

In front of my father and the man with the axe, there was a bed. As I walked around my father he took my hand. His hand was shaking. He did not look at me.

Agnes was lying on the bed in her old black coat. She had a torn-up night-dress on, under the coat. Her eyes were open. Her lips were blue. There were flies on her face. In her right hand was an empty bottle. On the wallpaper over her bed there were some words, written in crayon. "Oh, most sacred heart of Jesus, I place my trust in thee."

My father pulled me close to him for a moment. He held me tight. Then he made me turn away. "Go take care of your sisters and Rory," he said. "This isn't something you want them to see."

And when I turned away from him, that was when I saw them. The bottles.

On the floor. On the table. On a chair near the window. Under the bed. In the sink and the cooker. All over the kitchen. All the way up the stairs. My feet kicked against them. Sent them smashing down the steps and into the street. In the bath and around the toilet. Coke bottles. Gin bottles. Jam jars. Milk bottles. Plastic bottles in the shape of the Virgin Mary. An army of bottles, in Agnes Bernadette Graham's tiny flat.

The doctor said it was the damp. Everything in the house was soaked with damp. It was shocking, he said. It was no way for anyone to have to live. He pulled the dirty sheet up over Agnes's head. He sat on the chair and held her hand. Almost as though she was still alive.

Not many people came to her funeral. Just me and my father and Sheila and Helen. And little Rory in my father's arms. And this pretty young woman we didn't know, who said Agnes had once been very kind to her. But she didn't want to say exactly how.

My father gave a pound note to the

gravediggers. He said digging graves was hard work. A thing that wasn't easy for anyone to do. They nodded and said they were sorry for his trouble.

It was a sunny day, but very windy. So the priest's white lace robe kept blowing up into his face. I thought Agnes would have laughed if she'd seen that.

She really would have got a kick out of that.

Chapter Eight

The night of Agnes's funeral I couldn't sleep. I suppose that was around four months after my mother had gone.

When I came down the stairs it was very late. My father was sitting in the front room, in the armchair. He was still wearing his black suit from the funeral. His shoes were off, and his toes were sticking through his socks. And my father was crying.

His hands were kind of touching his face. He was softly saying a word to himself, over and over again. And the

word he was saying through his tears –
Rita, Rita, oh, Rita – was my mother's
name.

This wasn't the first time I had seen
my father cry. And it wasn't the last
time, not at all. But I think it was the
worst time. I really do.

He sat with his head in his hands.
He sat very still. Sobbing. Breathing
very hard. Saying my mother's name
over and over. As though my mother's
name was a poem, or maybe a prayer.

I wanted to cry too. Not just because
I was upset. But because I wanted to
cry with my father. I did not want him
to have to cry on his own. I wanted to
hold him. And for him to hold me. I
wanted to cry in his arms until our
tears had gone away. I could see in that
moment that my father had the right to
cry. And I wanted to cry too. But for
some reason I found that I couldn't.

A way I hadn't ever seen before. And he nodded a few times, as though he understood something.

"No," he said, quietly. "Well, you do."

And we sat in each other's arms then, watching *The Comedians*. Even when it was over we didn't move. We listened to the sound of the rain for a while, falling softly onto the street. I suppose we must have been thinking about all kinds of things. But I don't remember what things now. All I remember is the sound of the rain. And me, holding onto my father very hard.

I never saw my mother again. There was talk on the street that she had gone to England. A man said he had seen her in Cork. Another man said she was living in Galway. They read out her name on the radio news. The newsreader said she was a missing person. But even then, no word came. After a while people just stopped talking about her. It was like she had never lived in Glasthule at all.

My father got a job washing cars and doing odd jobs. He'd go around the rich houses in Killiney and Dalkey. He'd wash cars, he'd cut grass. Anything for a few pounds.

A man who had a huge posh house up in Dalkey paid my father to weed out and tidy his garden. It took him nearly three months to do it properly. Sometimes on Saturdays I would go and help him. I must say he did a lovely job.

The job was so good that the man paid my father to come back once a week and make sure the garden was all right. After a while, other people got to hear about it. My father was asked to do other gardens too. Funnily enough, that was work he seemed to like. He seemed to have a talent for it. He lost a bit of weight. His face got suntanned. He went to night-school and learned about plants.

In time he met another woman. She was a big fat biddy from the country and she laughed a lot. Her husband had died in a fire at his work. My father and her used to go walking the pier together. She drank a bit, but so did he. Some people said that was what kept them together. But talk is cheap. And nobody knows. Nobody can say what's going on in someone else's heart.

All I know myself is that she seemed to understand him. I think she made him very happy. They had awful rows sometimes but they always made up. She used to sing when she had a few drinks. Long, sad country-and-western songs. Irish ballads. "Danny Boy."

She'd sing on and on. She never stopped. She had a really awful voice too. My father said she had a voice that would peel a carrot. She was "a two bucket woman" my father said. She could drink two buckets of Guinness and come back for more. She'd suck the drink off a sore leg.

The last time I saw them together was at my sister Helen's wedding two years ago. After the dinner, my father got up to make a speech. He had everyone in stitches. He really did. His eyes were shining like little lumps of sunshine.

"Myself, I don't like the word marriage," he said. "In fact marriage isn't a word, it's a whole bloody sentence."

People laughed. He started to laugh himself. I think he must have got a fit of giggles. A thing a comedian should never do. You never laugh at your own jokes. Any comedian will tell you that. But that day, for some reason, my father did laugh. It was like he was happy, he really didn't care. It was like he had never had a worry in his life. He laughed until he was red in the face. Everyone laughed back. He laughed more. He roared with laughter. Everyone howled. Then he took a step backwards and fell right over. And everyone went mad, laughing and clapping.

I think they thought it was supposed to be funny. I think they thought it was part of his act. And that's the way he would have wanted it. You could say my father died laughing, in fact.

The church was packed with little old ladies for his funeral. The priest was new, he was a bit nervous. He said he had never met my father himself, but that everyone said he was a great comedian. And that he was also, in his shouted, down at the back. And everyone laughed, even the priest.

Sometimes even now I think I see him in the street. When I get the smell of bread he comes into my mind. And sometimes, at night, I think about him still. When I am tucking my own kids into bed. For some strange reason I often think of him then. Or whenever I see a comedian on the television, telling jokes and pulling faces. Sometimes just the sound of laughter brings him back. Like a ghost, I suppose. Or maybe just a memory.

I think about him walking Dun Laoghaire pier. Down to the lighthouse, looking out at the boats. And wishing he had gone away to England.

And then I picture him walking slowly back up. Along the seafront and back towards Glasthule. Laughing his

ITEM CHARGED

LIB#: *1000204345*
GRP: STUDENT

Due: 10/22/2012 08:00 PM

Title: Comedian / Joseph O'Connor.
Auth: O'Connor, Joseph, 1963-
Call #: 428.64 OCONNOR 2009
Enum
Chron
Copy:
Item *0068402K*

That was the night my childhood ended. Because when you have that feeling about your parents – that they, like you, have the right to cry – that is when you know you are not a child any more. In my life, that moment came very quickly. The way the biggest changes in your life can sometimes happen. In a way you wouldn't think would be important at all.

"Da," I said. "Don't be crying."

He looked up quickly. He was shocked to see me. I don't think he knew what to say for a while.

"I'm not," he said. "Why are you up?"

"You are," I said. "I saw you, Da."

"I'm not," he said. "I was thinking of something funny."

"Something funny?"

"Yes," he said. "People do that sometimes. When something is really gas, they get tears in their eyes. Crying with laughter is what it's called."

"So tell me a joke," I said to my father.

He thought for a while. He looked around the room.

"You wouldn't understand it," he said.

My father and I went into the kitchen. There was a packet of burgers sitting in the fridge. We fried them up with slices of stale bread. We sat in the front room, watching *The Comedians*. He drank a can of beer and I drank milk. He kept wiping his eyes with the back of his hand. Whenever he finished a cigarette, he lit another one on the end.

"I suppose you think your old da is an awful man now," he said. "I suppose you think he's a great big baby."

"No," I said. "That's not what I think."

"Yes, well, don't you worry about anything," he said. "You're too young to be worrying about the big things. We'll just keep the flag flying here. And things will work out for the best in the end."

"I won't worry," I said. "I promise."

He nodded and looked around the room.

"Do you know what I do when I get worried?" he said.

"No," I said. "What do you do?"

"I think about your great-great-grandfather. I think about the way he worked. All those huge stones. Them great big rocks. It must have been awful. Really and truly. There must have been days his back was half-broken. But in the end, you see, it was worth all the work. Because in the end, he was able to stand on the pier. He was able to say, "Look at this. I *did* something. I'm a man who did something with his life."

We sat in silence for a few minutes. The rain began to fall now, softly against the window of our house. Somewhere on the street a car alarm was going. All the old dogs were barking at the thunder.

My father looked at me and tried to smile. But the tears were running down his face again.

"Did I ever tell you," my father said suddenly, "that sometimes you look just like your mammy did. When she was young and we fell in love together."

"No," I said. "You never did."

My father bent his forehead. And he pinched his nose. He sat like that for a while and I watched him. And then slowly he raised his head again. He looked into my eyes in this strange way.

"Yes, well, don't you worry about anything," he said. "You're too young to be worrying about the big things. We'll just keep the flag flying here. And things will work out for the best in the end."

"I won't worry," I said. "I promise."

He nodded and looked around the room.

"Do you know what I do when I get worried?" he said.

"No," I said. "What do you do?"

"I think about your great-great-grandfather. I think about the way he worked. All those huge stones. Them great big rocks. It must have been awful. Really and truly. There must have been days his back was half-broken. But in the end, you see, it was worth all the work. Because in the end, he was able to stand on the pier. He was able to say, "Look at this. I *did*